Amber and Alfie

Alfie the kitten took a deep breath and leaped on to the train. "Amber, where are you?" he called urgently. At that moment he spotted the squirrel. She was right in the far corner, with her nose pushed into a small grey rucksack.

"Quick!" mewed Alfie. "Let's get out of here!"

But it was too late. The door slammed shut. Alfie heard the engine rumble even more loudly. The train had begun to move!

More Best Friends follow soon!

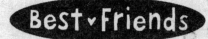

Best ♥ Friends

Amber and Alfie

by Jenny Dale

Illustrated by Susan Hellard

A Working Partners Book

MACMILLAN CHILDREN'S BOOKS

Special thanks to Jill Atkins

First published 2002 by Macmillan Children's Books
a division of Macmillan Publishers Limited
20 New Wharf Road, London N1 9RR
Basingstoke and Oxford
www.panmacmillan.com

Associated companies throughout the world

Created by Working Partners Limited
London W6 0QT

ISBN 0 330 41548 4

Text copyright © Working Partners Limited 2002
Illustrations copyright © Susan Hellard 2002
Best Friends is a trade mark of Working Partners Limited.

1 3 5 7 9 8 6 4 2

A CIP catalogue record for this book is available from
the British Library.

Typeset by SX Composing DTP, Rayleigh, Essex
Printed and bound in Great Britain by Mackays of Chatham plc, Kent

Chapter one

Amber, the red squirrel, peeped down through the branches of a pine tree. She could see her best friend, Alfie, the railway station kitten. He was trotting along the platform behind Mr Fuller, the stationmaster. Alfie's ginger fur showed up clearly against the white fence and the tubs of bright flowers.

Suddenly a pine needle pricked Amber's nose. "Ouch!" She sat back and rubbed her face. Then she crept forward and peeped down at Alfie again. He

1

hadn't noticed Amber sitting in the tree. She pulled a pine cone off the branch and dropped it on to the platform.

Alfie jumped as the pine cone landed beside him. He looked up at the tree. "Amber!" he mewed. "Was that you?" Amber was always up to mischief and playing games.

The wind rustled the branches of the tree, but Alfie couldn't see his friend anywhere. Maybe it wasn't Amber.

"Who threw that pine cone?" he called again. He arched his back and fluffed up his tail, trying to look fierce.

There was no reply. Alfie began to feel a bit silly. Maybe the wind had blown the pine cone off the tree after all! He sat down and began to lick his fur.

"That was a great trick!" Amber chuckled to herself.

Just then, a strong gust blew a shower of golden leaves down from a nearby beech tree. Amber dug her claws into the branches as the wind tugged at her fur. She watched the leaves flutter down to the platform.

Alfie jumped up. Those leaves were making his platform untidy! He pounced on the leaves one by one and picked them up in his mouth. Then he hid them behind a tub of flowers. The platform looked much tidier now.

Amber was beginning to feel a bit bored in the pine tree. She decided to climb down and play with Alfie.

"Look out, below!" she squeaked.

"Here I come!"

Quick as a flash, she leaped across to the beech tree. She clutched at the tip of a branch with all four paws. Her tummy fizzed with excitement as the branch swung up and down. When it finally stopped swaying, Amber scampered along it. She clawed her way around the trunk and scurried swiftly along another branch. Her bushy red tail streamed out behind her as she ran.

Down on the platform, she could see Alfie chasing another leaf. Amber dropped lightly on to the roof of a low stone building. This was where Mr Fuller sold tickets to people who wanted to ride up the mountain on the old steam train. Amber picked up a fallen beechnut and tossed it on to the platform. It landed right beside Alfie.

Alfie turned and flicked the nut with his front paw. It skidded through the fence and into the bushes behind the station. Just then, another nut came flying down.

"The wind is blowing down lots of

things today," he puffed. "It's making the station so untidy!"

He picked up the beechnut and tucked it behind the flower tub with the leaves. A big red flower nodded in the wind and tickled Alfie's nose. "Atishoo!" he sneezed. He patted the flower away and glanced along the platform. Good. It looked neat and tidy.

Amber chattered to herself with delight as she threw the third beechnut. This one bounced right off Alfie's head!

"Ouch!" Alfie miaowed. He looked up and saw a familiar squirrel face peering over the roof of the ticket office. "Oh, it's you, Amber! I haven't seen you all day. Have you been collecting food for the winter?"

"Yes," squeaked Amber. "I've found lots of tasty beechnuts, some hazelnuts and a few acorns. I've hidden them in my secret place."

"I bet your secret place is so secret you'll forget where it is!" joked Alfie.

"No I won't," Amber insisted. She threw another nut at him.

Alfie ducked. "Missed!" he mewed as three more beechnuts flew down on to the platform.

"Hey! Look at that," teased Amber, scampering along the edge of the roof. "Someone's been making your platform untidy!"

"Cheeky thing!" chuckled Alfie. He quickly tidied the nuts behind the tub with the others.

"Come and play with me, Alfie," squeaked Amber, twitching her bushy tail.

"I can't right now," Alfie told his friend. "I'm too busy!"

"You're *always* busy," Amber called.

"Of course I am," miaowed Alfie. "There's so much to do. I have to keep the platform tidy, say hello to the passengers *and* I've chased away two mice today."

"What would Mr Fuller do without you?" Amber teased. She sprang down and landed neatly on the platform.

Next to the ticket office was Mr Fuller's kitchen. Amber peeped into the ticket office. The door to the kitchen was open. She could see a yummy-looking bread roll on the table. Her nose twitched. Could she smell cheese? She darted through the doorway.

"You're not supposed to go in there!" Alfie called.

Amber jumped on to the table. The smell of cheese made her mouth water. "Yum, yum!" she squeaked. Her bushy tail quivered with excitement. She was just nibbling the edge of the roll when Alfie ran in.

"Hey!" he mewed, fluffing up his fur. "That belongs to Mr Fuller."

"But it's so tasty," mumbled Amber, her mouth full of breadcrumbs.

"Stop it!" Alfie miaowed.

"Winter will be here soon," Amber reminded him. "I need to eat lots of

food to keep me warm."

"But it's Mr Fuller's lunch," Alfie protested. Amber was so naughty!

"I'm sure he wouldn't mind if I had just a tiny bit."

"Yes, he would!"

At that moment, Alfie pricked up his ears. He had heard a click. He knew what that meant. It was the signal at the end of the platform. Alfie's whiskers twitched and he ran to the door. The train was coming!

chapter two

Alfie dashed outside. Mr Fuller was standing on the platform, wearing his smart blue cap. Alfie checked that there were no leaves or nuts to tidy away, then he bounded along to join Mr Fuller.

The train reached the station and steamed noisily towards them. The hot air ruffled Alfie's fur and made him blink. The shiny green engine gleamed brightly and the enormous silver wheels flashed in the sunshine. As the engine passed Alfie, it let out a gigantic cloud of steam. There was a screech of brakes and a loud hiss as the train stopped at the end of the platform.

Alfie loved the train. It came into the station several times every day and he knew the driver very well. He trotted along the platform and sprang up into the cab, keeping well away from the glowing fire. "Hello, Bert," he mewed.

Bert picked him up. "Hello, Alfie," he said, stroking Alfie's head with his grubby hand.

Alfie purred happily, keeping one eye on the platform over Bert's shoulder. Ted, the guard, was helping passengers off the train. Alfie felt very proud as he watched the happy passengers step on to his tidy platform. Just then, he noticed a girl carrying a rucksack arrive at the station. "I must go and say hello to her," he miaowed.

He wriggled free of the engine driver's arms. As he leaped down from the cab he caught sight of Amber hiding behind a flower tub. She was nibbling a chunk of bread roll.

"Put that back, Amber," Alfie miaowed. But Amber didn't hear him.

Mr Fuller opened a carriage door for the girl while she bent down to stroke Alfie. "Hello, kitty," she said. "Are you helping the stationmaster?"

"Of course," Alfie purred.

"We've been quite busy today, haven't we, Alfie?" said Mr Fuller. "Oh, I nearly forgot! I must fetch that birthday cake

for Ted." He lifted the girl's rucksack into the carriage and hurried away.

Alfie watched the girl climb into the train. When he looked around, Amber was no longer sitting behind the flower tub. "Where has she gone now?" he wondered.

From her hiding place under a chair, Amber watched Mr Fuller hurry through the ticket office and into the kitchen. He came out carrying a cardboard box. Amber's nose twitched. She could smell something really tasty. The yummy smell seemed to be coming from the box. "I wonder what's in there?" she chattered to herself.

Mr Fuller went back outside with the box. "I'll pop it in the guard's van so that Ted doesn't forget to take it home tonight," he said.

Amber slipped out from under the chair and scurried out of the door. Keeping to the back of the platform, she scampered after Mr Fuller. She dodged behind a tub of flowers and watched him put the box into the guard's van.

"Morning, Ted," Mr Fuller called to the guard, who was at the front of the train talking to the driver. Mr Fuller walked along the platform to join them.

Amber ran over to the guard's van. She stretched up on her back legs and peered in through the door. She sniffed. Yes! There was definitely something tasty in there.

It was quite dark inside the van.

Amber could make out the shapes of several boxes and a bicycle. She wondered which one was Mr Fuller's box. She glanced back along the platform. Nobody had noticed her. Quick as a flash, she sprang up through the doorway and started to sniff at each of the boxes.

"All set?" asked Mr Fuller as he walked over to Alfie.

"Yes," miaowed Alfie, rubbing his head against Mr Fuller's legs.

Suddenly a tiny movement caught Alfie's eye. He looked round. Amber's bright red tail was just disappearing into the guard's van. "Oh, no!" wailed Alfie. "Amber, come out of there! The train's about to leave!"

But Amber was nowhere to be seen. Alfie dashed towards the guard's van just as Ted was about to close the door. "Wait!" Alfie mewed in alarm. "Don't go yet!"

Ted turned towards Mr Fuller. "All ready?" he called.

"Yes," Mr Fuller called back. "See you next time."

Alfie peered into the guard's van. "Amber!" he mewed, but there was no sign of her. Ted had his hand on the door handle. He was still talking to Mr Fuller, so he didn't notice Alfie standing on his back legs, looking into the van.

Alfie took a deep breath and leaped into the van. He skidded on the smooth floor and scrabbled madly with his paws.

He stopped with a bump against a large box. "Amber, where are you?" he called urgently. At that moment, he spotted the squirrel. She was right in the far corner, with her nose pushed into a small grey rucksack.

"Quick!" mewed Alfie. "Let's get out of here!"

But it was too late. The door slammed shut. Alfie heard the engine rumble even more loudly. He felt a jolt and sat down hard on his bottom. The train had begun to move!

chapter three

Alfie jumped as the train shuddered and clanked with the effort of moving. He leaped on to a cardboard box and stared out of the window. The train was rolling along the platform, past the ticket office. It went faster and faster until the white railings flashed past in a blur and the station whizzed out of sight.

"Oh dear," mewed Alfie. "What are we going to do now?"

Amber was too busy to answer. She was digging eagerly in the rucksack. She hadn't found Mr Fuller's box, but something in here smelled almost as good.

"I'm not supposed to get *on* the train!" Alfie miaowed. He was very frightened. The train was taking him further and further away from home!

"Oh, yummy!" Amber rolled an apple out of the rucksack and began to nibble at the juicy fruit. She couldn't understand why Alfie was making a fuss. She quite liked the way the train rocked and rumbled.

"Mr Fuller will be wondering where I am," mewed Alfie.

"Don't worry," Amber mumbled through a mouthful of apple. "Come and share these tasty snacks."

23

"You shouldn't have come in here," Alfie said crossly. He jumped down from the box and sniffed inside the rucksack.

"Nor should you," answered Amber as she took another bite of crunchy apple.

"I was trying to warn you that the train was leaving," mewed Alfie.

"I didn't hear you," Amber replied.

"You were too busy searching for food, as usual," Alfie grumbled. But he couldn't feel cross with Amber for long. He had just found a paper bag with a ham sandwich in it. He ripped the paper open with his claws and pulled out some ham from the middle of the sandwich. It was really tasty!

Alfie swallowed the last mouthful of ham and licked his face and paws clean.

Then he leaped back on to the box. His tummy flipped with excitement. Snow-capped mountains towered above them. "Wow!" he miaowed. "Look at this!"

Amber jumped up beside Alfie. "Wow!' she echoed. "Look at all those trees! I bet there's enough food for lots and lots of winters in there!" She sprang up on to a wire shelf that stretched beneath the window. "Hey! You can see even better from up here. Come and look."

Alfie jumped up beside her. Amber reached over and playfully tweaked his tail. "Isn't this exciting?" she squeaked.

All at once, Amber's nose twitched. It was that yummy smell again. She remembered why she had crept into the

25

guard's van. "Now, where did Mr Fuller put that box?" she wondered.

She jumped down to the floor and sniffed again. With her tail held high, she followed the smell past the bicycle and around the grey rucksack. Behind the rucksack was a big white box, just like the one Mr Fuller had been carrying.

Amber's mouth watered. She pushed her nose under the lid and lifted it up. Inside there was a big round cake, covered in yellow icing. Amber leaned in and had a lick. The icing was very sticky, but it tasted wonderful!

Alfie settled down on the wire shelf and stared out of the window. The train was travelling fast now. Tall, dark-green trees sped past in a blur. A break in the trees revealed a sparkling waterfall tumbling down the side of the mountain.

Just then, the train began to slow down. Alfie pressed his cheek against the window. He could see a white fence and the end of a platform. They must be coming to another station.

Alfie had a brilliant idea. "Hey!" he called down to Amber. "If we get off here, we can wait on the platform for another train going back to our station."

"I suppose so," mumbled Amber. She looked up at Alfie with cake crumbs stuck to her whiskers. "But I wish I could take this lovely cake back to my winter store."

"As soon as the train stops," Alfie purred, dropping down from the shelf, "we'll slip out on to the platform and find somewhere to hide until the next train comes to take us home."

"OK," squeaked Amber, licking the crumbs from her paws.

Alfie stood with his nose pressed against the door. Amber crouched behind him. There was a shrill whistle from the engine, then a loud hiss of steam. The train shuddered to a stop. They heard Ted walking towards the guard's van. He was coming to take out the luggage.

"Ready?" Alfie mewed, getting ready to jump.

Ted slid open the door and bright

sunlight flooded in. Alfie and Amber blinked. "Now!" Alfie miaowed. He slipped out of the door and on to the platform.

At once a shadow loomed above him, blocking the way.

"Woof!"

Alfie dug in his claws and skidded to a halt. Right in front of him was the biggest, fiercest dog he had ever seen!

———

chapter four

Amber was so close behind Alfie that she couldn't stop in time. She slid straight into him. Thump! Amber hid her head under her paws, hoping the dog would go away. It was barking very loudly. "Help!" she whimpered.

Alfie could feel Amber trembling against him. He felt a bit braver because he wanted to look after his friend. He fluffed up his fur and arched his back. "Go away!" he hissed to the big brown dog.

"Woof! Woof!" barked the dog.

Alfie hissed again, but the dog growled and took a step towards him. Alfie realised there was only one thing to do. "Get back into the train, Amber!" he mewed.

Quick as lightning, they leaped back into the guard's van. They scrambled into a corner and hid behind a large box. The dog stood outside, barking fiercely.

"Quiet, Butch!" shouted Ted from the platform.

Amber felt her heart pounding. That dog was so scary! She could hear Alfie panting beside her. He must be frightened too. Amber nudged him with her nose to make him feel better.

After a while, the dog stopped barking.

Amber heard the guard lifting out the
bicycle. She tucked in her tail so he
would not see her behind the box. When
the guard had gone, she crept to the
open door and peered out.

"Is it safe?" mewed Alfie.

"The dog's gone," squeaked Amber.

"Good," mewed Alfie. "Let's get out
of here before it comes back."

He was just about to join Amber at the door when they heard voices. It sounded like children talking and laughing.

Amber leaned out of the guard's van. She saw a long line of children walking along the platform. "Keep down, Alfie!" she chattered, backing away from the door.

"Right," called Ted. "You can put your rucksacks in here."

A boy appeared in the doorway. He flung a bright red rucksack into the guard's van. Amber leaped back out of the way just in time.

"Look out!" warned Alfie as another rucksack flew in.

Amber scrambled behind the birthday-cake box. The bag whizzed

34

towards her and thumped down on top
of the box. "Hey!" Amber squeaked.
"You've squashed my cake!" Then two
more children threw in their bags. "It's
getting dangerous in here!" puffed
Amber. She scurried over to Alfie. They
huddled together behind a big box, out
of the way of flying rucksacks.

At last, the bags stopped coming in.

Alfie could hear the children laughing and shouting as they walked along the platform to the next carriage. Then he heard a whistle, just like Mr Fuller's.

"Quick, Amber, the train's about to leave!" he miaowed. But before they could escape on to the platform, Ted slammed the door again. The train jolted and began to move.

"Oh, help!" cried Alfie. "We're in big trouble now! We're going even further away from home."

Amber sprang up on to the wire shelf and looked closely at the window. "If I could just get this window open," she squeaked, "I could scramble up on to the roof. I might be able to see where we are going."

"Good idea," mewed Alfie as he jumped up to join her. "But be careful, it could be dangerous."

"Don't worry," Amber squeaked. "I'm a good climber – all squirrels are."

She began gnawing away at the wooden window frame. She had just managed to open the window a little way when there was a rush of wind and a loud rattling roar, and everything suddenly went black!

Chapter five

Amber crouched on the shelf and gripped the wire tightly. She knew Alfie was still beside her. Although she could not see him, she could feel him shaking. What had happened? It had never been as dark as this before, even at night-time!

Alfie huddled close to Amber. His ears were flat and his fur was fluffed up. He opened his eyes very wide but it was so dark he couldn't see anything. The train rocked and rolled, zooming through the darkness. It went on and on for such a

long time that he began to think it would
never end.

Suddenly, brilliant sunshine burst into
the guard's van and the roaring stopped.
Alfie blinked and sat up. He sighed with
relief as he looked around him. They
were still sitting on the shelf with boxes
and rucksacks below them. "What was
that?" he mewed to Amber.

The red squirrel shook her head, her
eyes wide with alarm. "I don't know,"
she replied. She started nibbling and
scratching at the window frame again.
"Look, it's opening!" she squeaked.

Alfie used his sharp claws to help her.
Soon the glass pane slid further down.
"Can you squeeze through that gap?"
Alfie panted.

"I'll try," squeaked Amber. She wriggled and pushed her body through the window.

"Mind you don't fall," warned Alfie as he watched her scramble up the side of the train. The last thing he saw was her long red tail blowing in the wind. Then she disappeared over the edge, on to the roof.

Amber knew she had to hold on tightly. The wind was very strong up here and the train was moving fast. The wind ruffled her fur and felt tickly along her back.

She took a few careful steps across the roof. It was much smoother than the rough bark of tree branches, so she clung on tightly with her claws to stop

herself slipping. She looked back at the way they had come. The shiny railway track came straight out of a round black hole in the mountain. The train must have been inside that hole!

Amber leaned over the side of the roof and hung upside-down above the window. "You'll never guess what," she squeaked to Alfie. "I think we've been inside the mountain. There's a dark hole, and the track comes out of it!"

Alfie looked at Amber's upside-down face outside the window. He put his head on one side so that her face looked almost the right way up. "Wow!" he miaowed. "We've really been inside the mountain?"

"It looks like it!"

"What about the next station?" Alfie called. "Can you see it yet?"

Amber swung herself back on to the roof. She looked at the big green engine with white smoke billowing from it. Ahead of the train, the track disappeared around another mountain. There was no sign of a station.

Just then, Amber noticed a tasty-looking hazelnut rolling around in a ridge on the roof of the next carriage. Her mouth watered. There was a space between the carriage and the guard's van, but she was sure she could jump across. She had jumped much further between trees at home.

Amber crept forward and peered down into the gap. She saw the rails flashing below. It looked dangerous down there. She would really have to make sure she didn't fall. The train rattled and rocked, but Amber found her balance and crouched, ready to spring. Then she took a flying leap across the gap. She grabbed on to the edge of the carriage roof as she landed and pulled herself up. She reached out for the nut but, suddenly, the train jolted and the nut rolled out of her reach. Amber crawled towards it. Then, above the whistling of the wind in her ears, she heard the children again. Their voices seemed to be coming from underneath her.

Amber peered over the edge of the roof and looked in through the window below. Several children stared back up at her.

"Look, Miss Hart! There's a squirrel on the roof!" one of them shouted.

"Don't be silly," said the teacher from inside the carriage. "Of course there isn't!"

"There is! Look!"

Back inside the guard's van, Alfie wondered where Amber had got to. He could hear the children shouting. He poked his head through the opening in the window. Whoosh! The wind blew his ears inside out and ruffled his whiskers. Forcing his eyes open against the wind, Alfie could just see some children peering out of the next carriage.

"Ben, Jody, come back inside!" called the teacher. "It's very dangerous to lean out of the window when the train is moving." The faces disappeared from the window, back into the carriage.

Up on the roof, Amber tried to grab the hazelnut. It skidded out of reach and dropped over the side of the carriage. Amber chattered crossly to herself. But by now the train had gone round the mountain, and she could see some buildings ahead, by the side of the track. Was it another station? Amber scampered back on to the roof of the guard's van.

Alfie jumped as Amber slipped back through the window. Her fur was sticking up in all directions and her eyes were wide with excitement. "I tried to bring you a hazelnut," she panted. "But it rolled off the roof."

"Lucky it was the nut and not you," mewed Alfie, screwing up his nose. "Anyway, cats don't like nuts. Did you see a station while you were up on the roof?"

"Yes, I think so," Amber squeaked.

"Good," miaowed Alfie.

At that moment, there was a loud
whistle and the train began to slow
down. Alfie pressed his cheek against the
window and peered out. He could see a
platform with some tubs of bright-
coloured flowers and a white fence. "It
looks quite safe," he mewed. "There's
no dog."

The train slowed to a stop. Alfie leaped down from the rack and stood by the door. As soon as it slid open, he peeped out. "All clear!" he called to Amber, who was crouching behind him. "Quick! Let's hide behind that tub of flowers."

He took a deep breath. Maybe this time they would find a train to take them home? Amber and Alfie jumped out of the train, raced across the platform and fell in a panting heap behind the flower tub.

chapter six

Amber had just tucked her tail out of sight when the carriage door opened and the children began to pour out.

"We saw a red squirrel on top of the train!" one girl said to Ted.

"You're pulling my leg!" exclaimed the guard.

"We're not!" said another.

Ted craned his neck and peered up at the roof. "Well, it's not there now!"

Alfie and Amber crouched down low while the children trooped past and out of the station. Alfie glanced around him. The tub of flowers looked exactly the same as the one at his station. There was even a pile of leaves and beechnuts tucked behind the tub, like the ones he had tidied away. Just then, the wind blew and a big red flower bent down and tickled his nose. "Atishoo!" Alfie sneezed. That was funny. He could remember

being tickled like that before . . .

Amber picked up a beechnut and began to nibble it. "Yum!" she mumbled. "I wonder if another squirrel left these here?"

The platform was quiet now, so Alfie peeped out from behind the tub. The station looked *very* familiar. He saw the ticket office and the waiting room and … Mr Fuller's office! The train had brought them back to *his* station.

"Amber!" he purred happily. "We're home!"

At that moment, Mr Fuller came out of the office. He looked worried.

"What's the matter?" asked Ted, who was unloading some parcels.

"I can't find Alfie. Have you seen him

anywhere?" said Mr Fuller.

"No," said Ted. "Not since I was here this morning."

"Well, keep an eye out for him, will you?" said Mr Fuller sadly.

Ted went over to the guard's van and leaned in. "Oh no!" he said, turning round with the cake box in his hands. "Look at my birthday cake. It's all squashed."

"What a shame!" said Mr Fuller.

Ted frowned. "And I think it's been *nibbled*!" he said. "Who could have done that?" He glanced up at the roof of the train and shook his head. Then he shrugged and put the squashed box back into the van. He climbed on board.

The train chuffed noisily out of the

station and Mr Fuller walked back into his office.

When he had gone, Amber popped out from her hiding place. "We're back!" she squeaked, chasing her tail until she was giddy.

Alfie raced along the platform and into the office. "Mr Fuller!" he mewed, as loudly as he could. "I'm home!"

A big smile spread across Mr Fuller's face as he picked Alfie up and hugged him. "Hello, my little helper," he said. "I've been worried about you. I thought you'd got lost."

"Oh no," purred Alfie, snuggling against Mr Fuller's chest. "Amber and I have been on a train journey, but we're glad to be home now."

"I've got your favourite treat for your tea," said Mr Fuller. "Sardines."

Alfie licked his lips. "Yum!" he mewed.

Mr Fuller carried him through the office and into the kitchen. "Here you are," he said, putting Alfie down on the floor beside a dish of sardines.

Alfie tucked in. His adventure had made him very hungry. Out of the corner of his eye, he saw a familiar red face peeping in at the door.

"What's that?" Amber asked.

"Sardines," Alfie replied. "Would you like one?"

Amber wrinkled up her nose. "No, thanks. Squirrels don't like sardines!" She lifted her paw and showed Alfie a beechnut. "I've brought my own snack from behind the tub of flowers. It's lucky I threw this at you this morning!" And she cracked open the shell to get at the tasty nut inside.

When she had finished, she nuzzled Alfie's face. "We had a great adventure, didn't we?" she asked. "I wasn't scared at all, were you?"

"Oh no," mumbled Alfie through a

mouthful of sardine. Then he saw a
twinkle in Amber's eye. "Well, maybe a
bit scared. Anyway, I'm not going on any
more train journeys. Mr Fuller needs me
to stay here and help him!" He licked his
paws and cleaned his whiskers.

"And I need to find some more nuts
for my winter store," Amber squeaked.
She dashed out of the door. "Bet you

can't catch me!" she called over her shoulder.

Alfie jumped to his feet and chased her out on to the platform. He checked the signal. It was up. That meant there was no train coming. There was plenty of time to play with his friend before the next train was due!

Collect all of JENNY DALE BEST FRIENDS!

The prices shown below are correct at the time of going to press. However, Macmillan Publishers reserve the right to show new retail prices on covers which may differ from those previously advertised.

JENNY DALE'S BEST FRIENDS

1. Snowflake and Sparkle	0 330 39853 9	£3.50
2. Pogo and Pip	0 330 39854 7	£3.50
3. Minty and Monty	0 330 39855 5	£3.50
4. Carrot and Clover	0 330 39856 3	£3.50
5. Bramble and Berry	0 330 39857 1	£3.50
6. Blossom and Beany	0 330 39775 3	£3.50
7. Skipper and Sky	0 330 41545 X	£3.50
8. Amber and Alfie	0 330 415548 4	£3.50

All Macmillan titles can be ordered at your local bookshop or are available by post from:

Book Service by Post
PO Box 29, Douglas, Isle of Man IM99 1BQ

Credit cards accepted. For details:
Telephone: 01624 675137
Fax: 01624 670923
E-mail: bookshop@enterprise.net

Free postage and packing in the UK.
Overseas customers: add £1 per book (paperback)
and £3 per book (hardback).